jj   6/08

        Kung Fu Panda.

                    DISCARD

HarperCollins®, ☷®, and HarperEntertainment™
are trademarks of HarperCollins Publishers.
Kung Fu Panda: The Movie Storybook
Kung Fu Panda ™ & © 2008 DreamWorks Animation L.L.C.
Printed in the United States of America. All rights reserved.
No part of this book may be used or reproduced in any manner
whatsoever without written permission except in the case of brief
quotations embodied in critical articles and reviews.
For information address HarperCollins Children's Books, a division of
HarperCollins Publishers, 1350 Avenue of the Americas, New York, NY 10019.
www.harpercollinschildrens.com
Library of Congress catalog card number: 2008922485
ISBN 978-0-06-143464-8
Book design by Rick Farley
❖
First Edition

DREAMWORKS

KUNG FU PANDA

THE MOVIE STORYBOOK

Adapted by Catherine Hapka
Pencils by Marcelo Matere
Paintings by Justin Gerard

HarperEntertainment
An Imprint of HarperCollinsPublishers

Legend told of a mighty kung fu warrior who traveled throughout the Valley of Peace, protecting the innocent in his supercool way.

Fighting ninjas and battling criminals, this kung fu warrior was so deadly that his enemies sometimes went blind before his pure awesomeness.

Even the greatest warriors, the Furious Five, bowed in respect to the Dragon Warrior's power and skill. . . .

"Po! Get up! You'll be late for work!" Po's father yelled up the stairs.

Po sat up in bed. He had been dreaming! He wasn't the Dragon Warrior after all. He was just a large, sleepy panda.

He rushed downstairs to his father's noodle shop. The shop was crowded with customers who loved his father's secret-ingredient noodle soup. As Po struggled to squeeze and fit between the tables, he was still thinking about his dream. It would be great to be a real kung fu warrior who sent his enemies flying. . . .

Oops! Po's belly sent the tables in the noodle shop flying instead.

Meanwhile, at the Jade Palace, Shifu was training the Furious Five when Master Oogway summoned him.

"I have had a vision," Oogway said. "Tai Lung will return."

Tai Lung had once been Shifu's star pupil but he had grown overly ambitious. When he tried to steal the Dragon Scroll and its secret to unlimited power, Oogway and Shifu had stopped him. Now, Tai Lung had been locked away in prison for years.

Shifu was concerned—he knew that Oogway's visions were never wrong. It was time to plan for Tai Lung's return.

Word of the plan spread quickly. That very day, Oogway would choose the Dragon Warrior—the mighty kung fu master destined to save the Valley from Tai Lung.

"This is the greatest day in kung fu history!" Po cried when he heard the news. He had to be there to see which of the Furious Five would be chosen.

He ran up the arena stairs with all his might, panting and sweating. He finally reached the top, just to see the doors slam in his face—*whoosh!* He tried to pole-vault over the wall. Then he tried to climb. But *nothing* worked . . . until he shot himself high into the air with some fireworks.

SPLAT!

Po landed inside the arena. When he looked up, he saw that Master Oogway was pointing at him. Master Shifu and the Furious Five were staring down at him.

"The universe has brought us the Dragon Warrior," Oogway declared. The crowd cheered in celebration of the news.

"What?" Po said in surprise.

"What?" exclaimed Shifu and the Five in disbelief.

Soon Po found himself in the Sacred Hall of Heroes. It was the coolest place he'd ever seen. Ancient kung fu artifacts were displayed throughout the room. Po ran around checking out all of them.

"Hel–loooo!" he called into the Urn of Whispering Warriors.

"Have you finished sightseeing?" a voice asked.

Po gasped. The urn was talking to him!

"Would you turn around?" the voice said.

Po turned around. "Master Shifu!" he cried when he saw the kung fu master. So *that* was who was talking to him! Po was so surprised that he bumped into the urn. It shattered into dozens of tiny pieces. "Um, do you have some glue?" he asked sheepishly.

Shifu wasn't at all impressed with this new so-called Dragon Warrior. He tested Po by putting him into the Wuxi Finger Hold.

It really, really hurt. But Po still thought it was pretty cool.

Shifu took Po to the training hall where the Five were practicing. Masters Tigress, Monkey, Crane, Viper, and Mantis performed death-defying kung fu stunts. Po was thrilled to see his heroes in action.

Po was less thrilled when he realized *he* was supposed to join in.

"Go ahead, panda," Shifu said. "Show us what you can do."

Po was flung into the gauntlet as: *OUCH!* A spiky tethered ball sent Po flying into the jade exercise, which *OOF!* spilled him into the army of wooden dummies, when *UGH!* he got whacked for a final time, landing beaten-up in front of the disapproving Five.

Po didn't fit in at the training hall, and he didn't fit in at the Furious Five's bunkhouse. None of the Five wanted him around. They didn't think he was worthy of being the Dragon Warrior.

Feeling dejected, Po wandered outside to a peach tree. How could Shifu ever turn someone like *him* into a kung fu hero?

"Maybe I should just quit and go back to making noodles," he mumbled sadly.

Master Oogway overheard the panda's sad words and gave him some advice. "Yesterday is history, tomorrow is a mystery, but today is a gift. That is why it is the present," said Oogway. Po smiled. He was willing to try again.

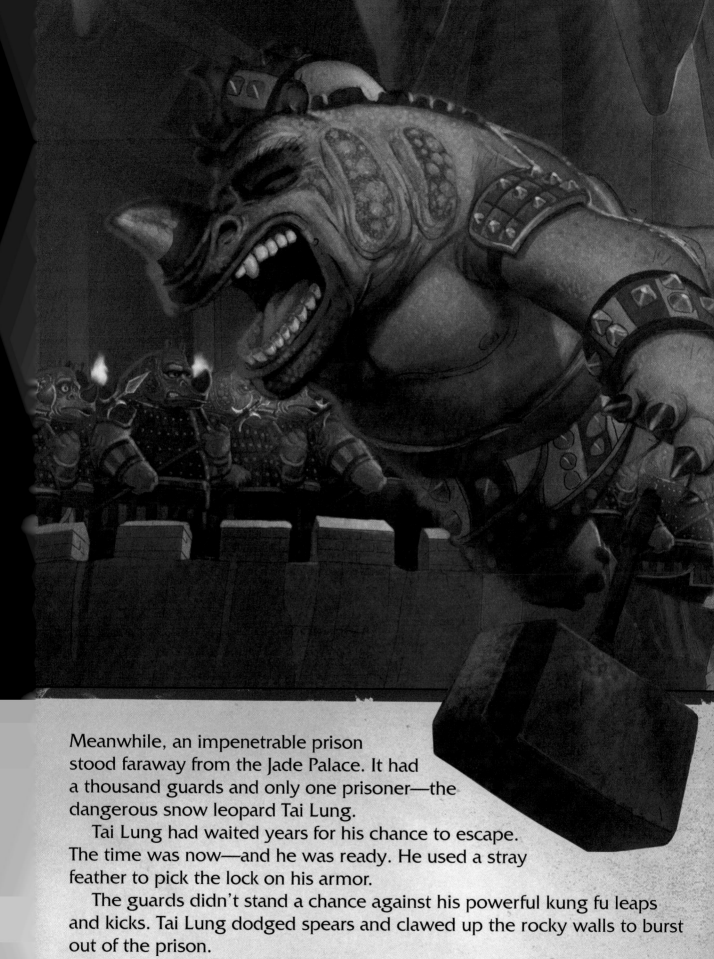

Meanwhile, an impenetrable prison
stood faraway from the Jade Palace. It had
a thousand guards and only one prisoner—the
dangerous snow leopard Tai Lung.

Tai Lung had waited years for his chance to escape.
The time was now—and he was ready. He used a stray
feather to pick the lock on his armor.

The guards didn't stand a chance against his powerful kung fu leaps
and kicks. Tai Lung dodged spears and clawed up the rocky walls to burst
out of the prison.

At last, he was free! Now he could return to the palace and claim his
rightful title of Dragon Warrior!

Back at the palace, Po was training hard with the Five. First Viper flipped him ears over heels and sent him crashing down on his head.

"That was awesome!" Po cried. "Let's go again!"

Next it was Monkey's turn. He whacked Po all over his chubby body with a bamboo cane. Then Crane sent Po falling flat on his face.

Shifu was fed up. "I've been taking it easy on you, panda," he said. "Your next opponent will be . . . me!"

He grabbed Po in a kung fu hold. "The path to victory is to use your opponent's strength against him until he fails or quits," he said.

Po was inspired. "Don't worry, Master. I will never quit!"

But time was running out for Po to master kung fu. The bad news about Tai Lung's escape reached the palace. Shifu rushed to tell Oogway.

"That *is* bad news," Oogway said. "*If* you do not believe that the Dragon Warrior can stop him."

"Master, that panda is not the Dragon Warrior!" Shifu cried.

"You just need to believe, Shifu," Oogway told him. "Now you must continue your journey without me."

He handed his staff to Shifu. Then he backed away and disappeared forever in a swirl of petals. . . .

Back at the bunkhouse, Po was making the Furious Five laugh by imitating Shifu when Shifu himself suddenly walked in.

"Tai Lung is coming," he told Po sternly. "You are the only one who can stop him."

"What?" Po cried. He laughed nervously. "And here I thought you had no sense of humor. *I'm* going to stop Tai Lung?"

But he realized that Shifu was serious. As soon as the master turned to speak to the Five, Po spun on his heel and ran away as fast as he could. Shifu soon caught up with Po. His message was clear.

"I can train you," Shifu said. "I will turn you into the Dragon Warrior."

Tigress was sure Po could never defeat Tai Lung. She sneaked out of the bunkhouse that night to do the job herself. The others chased after her.

"Don't try to stop me," she warned them.

"We're not trying to stop you," Viper said. "We're coming with you!"

The Furious Five found Tai Lung on a rope bridge spanning a vast gorge.

The Five began their attack. They fought bravely, just as Shifu had taught them.

But the snow leopard's strong muscles backed up his kung fu kicks as he overpowered the group, finally using a special kung fu nerve attack that froze them in place. Tai Lung snarled as he bounded away to the Valley.

Back at the palace, Shifu found Po eating everything he could get his paws on. Finally Shifu understood. *This* was the key to the panda's greatness!

Shifu changed his training plans. He would use food not to motivate Po— but to activate him! Instead of the usual kung fu methods, he used stir-fry and dumplings to build and refine Po's skills.

It worked! Po got better and better.

Po was excited. His kung fu dreams were coming true at last. Maybe he *was* worthy of being the Dragon Warrior after all!

The Five returned, dejected, and told Shifu of their defeat to Tai Lung. Shifu decided that Po needed to meet his destiny head-on—he needed the Dragon Scroll.

"Read it, Po, and fulfill your destiny," he said. "Read it and become the Dragon Warrior!"

Po unrolled the scroll and gasped. "It's blank!"

All his new confidence seeped away. Tai Lung had already defeated the Five. How was a chubby, noodle-slurping panda ever supposed to beat him? Even Shifu didn't understand.

When Shifu ordered an evacuation of the Valley, Po went straight to his father's noodle shop. His father quickly realized that Po needed some encouragement. And so he finally revealed the secret ingredient in his special noodle soup.

"There *is* no secret ingredient," he told Po. "To make something special, you just have to *believe* it's special."

Po was shocked. "There is no secret ingredient," he said to himself.

He unrolled the blank scroll again and saw his own reflection in the shiny surface. It all made sense—there *was* no secret of the scroll. Now Po understood what he had to do!

When Tai Lung arrived at the palace, Shifu was waiting for him.

"I have come home, Master," Tai Lung said.

"This is no longer your home," Shifu replied. "And I am no longer your master."

They began a fierce fight. Shifu was a great kung fu master, but Tai Lung was now too strong for him.

Po burst into the palace just as Tai Lung was about to make a final, deadly move on Shifu. At first Tai Lung couldn't believe it: *This* chubby panda was the Dragon Warrior?

"What are you going to do, big guy?" he taunted. "Sit on me?"

But Po didn't use the same kung fu moves as other warriors . . . he had his own panda style. The battle raged down the palace steps and through the village. The panda bounced the bad guy off his big belly.

When the dust settled, Po jumped up and snatched Tai Lung's finger. "Not the Wuxi Finger Hold!" yelled Tai Lung. The panda flexed his pinky, and it was all over. The Dragon Warrior had won.

Cheers rang out from every direction as Po marched victoriously through the Valley.

Shifu could hardly believe it. "It is as Oogway foretold," he said. "You are the Dragon Warrior. Thank you, Po!" The Five bowed with respect.

Po couldn't stop smiling. It was great that everyone finally believed he was truly the Dragon Warrior. But it was even better believing in himself!